PUFFIN BOOKS

FREAKY FAMILIES

# Cousin Cedric Goes Bananas

Karen Wallace was born in Canada and spent her childhood messing about on the river in the backwoods of Quebec. Now she lives in Herefordshire with her husband – the author Sam Llewellyn – two sons and a cat called Cougar.

*Some other books by Karen Wallace*

FREAKY FAMILIES: GREAT-AUNT IRIS GOES HUNTING

CREAKIE HALL: ACE GHOSTS
CREAKIE HALL: GHOULS RULE
CREAKIE HALL: STAR SPOOKS
CREAKIE HALL: FUNKY PHANTOMS

Karen Wallace

# Cousin Cedric Goes Bananas

Illustrated by Colin Paine

PUFFIN BOOKS

PUFFIN BOOKS

Published by the Penguin Group
Penguin Books Ltd, 27 Wrights Lane, London W8 5TZ, England
Penguin Putnam Inc., 375 Hudson Street, New York, New York 10014, USA
Penguin Books Australia Ltd, Ringwood, Victoria, Australia
Penguin Books Canada Ltd, 10 Alcorn Avenue, Toronto, Ontario, Canada M4V 3B2
Penguin Books (NZ) Ltd, Private Bag 102902, NSMC, Auckland, New Zealand

Penguin Books Ltd, Registered Offices: Harmondsworth, Middlesex, England

First published 1999
1 3 5 7 9 10 8 6 4 2



Printed in Hong Kong by Midas Printing Ltd



British Library Cataloguing in Publication Data
A CIP catalogue record for this book is available from the British Library

ISBN 0–140–38500–2

# 1. Something Peculiar

Mrs Primly-Proper was having a bad day. Every time she hung out the washing, hailstones crashed down on her head and gave her a headache. Every time she swept the leaves off the patio, a tiny tornado swirled through the garden and blew them all over the lawn.

"There's something peculiar going on," declared Mrs Primly-Proper.

"Here's something peculiar," said Mr Primly-Proper. He held up a letter in his hand. "Cousin Cedric wants Jack and Daisy to visit him."

"Cousin Cedric?" cried Jack and Daisy in dismay.

Now, that really *was* peculiar.

Jack looked at Daisy.

Daisy looked at Jack.

They had only met Cousin Cedric once. He was a dusty little man who worked in a museum. He spent his time reading old books and rolls of flaky, yellow paper.

Cousin Cedric said they were called scrolls and they were very old and very important. Jack and Daisy thought they looked as if he had found them in a dustbin.

"Cousin Cedric's an oddball," said Daisy.

"Cousin Cedric's a weirdo," said Jack.

"Cousin Cedric is an *Egyptologist*," said Mr Primly-Proper, primly. "He knows all about pyramids and mummies."

"What?"

"You'll see when you get to Egypt," said Mr Primly-Proper. He waved a small shiny folder. "These are your aeroplane tickets."

Jack and Daisy felt a strange tingling in their stomachs. Aeroplanes were too exciting for words!

"But what happens when we get there?" asked Daisy. Aeroplanes were fun, but airports were big busy places and rather frightening.

Mr Primly-Proper patted Daisy on the shoulder. "Don't worry, dear," he said with a smile. "Cousin Cedric will be there to meet you."

# 2. Can You Ride a Camel?

When Jack and Daisy arrived in Egypt, they couldn't see Cousin Cedric anywhere. There were young boys carrying trays of shining bracelets and glittering necklaces. There were women balancing trays of tiny, coloured cakes on their heads. And there was a huge man with a thick black beard and a monkey on his shoulders.

But there was no one who looked at all like Cousin Cedric.

"What are we going to do?" said Daisy nervously. As she spoke, the monkey ran across the room and began to pull at her sock.

A moment later, the huge man with the black beard stood in front of them.

"Are you, by any chance, Jack and Daisy Primly-Proper?"

At first, Jack and Daisy were too stunned to speak. They were sure this man wasn't their Cousin Cedric, but how did he know who they were?

"Don't be surprised," said the man, smiling. "Albert is never wrong."

"Albert?" said Daisy.

The big man pointed to the monkey and gave it a peanut. "Albert Einstein, of course! He knows everything. But come!" The big man held out his hand. "You are getting confused. I am Amed, a friend of your Cousin Cedric."

Amed looked at his watch. "He said he would be a minute late and I was to meet you." Amed smiled again and winked at Daisy. "Airports can be frightening places sometimes."

"They certainly can," said Daisy, feeling better already.

Exactly a minute later, a man

wearing round spectacles, a scarlet-and-gold headdress and white flowing robes strode towards them.

"Greetings!" said the man. "I am your Cousin Cedric."

"You are?" cried Jack and Daisy in astonishment.

"I am," said Cousin Cedric.

"But you're wearing a funny hat," cried Jack. Then he blushed because Daisy had kicked his shin. "Er, I mean, I like your hat."

"Thank you," replied Cousin Cedric, grinning. He turned to Amed and they exchanged looks. "You will be there at the appointed hour?"

"Indeed, I will," said Amed, bowing gravely.

He said goodbye to Jack and Daisy and turned away.

Jack stared as the huge man disappeared into the crowd.

"Who –"

But Cousin Cedric held up his hand for silence. "Before we go any further, I must ask you two questions."

He peered at Jack and Daisy from behind his spectacles. "Can you keep a secret?" he said solemnly.

"Yes!" cried Jack and Daisy.

"Can you ride a camel?"

"No!" cried Jack and Daisy.

"If you can do one, you can learn the other," replied Cousin Cedric. "As for Amed, he is my friend and my assistant and he drives a very fast car! Now follow me!"

And without another word, Cousin Cedric strode off, his scarlet-and-gold headdress sparkling in the sun.

# 3. A Thunderstorm in the Desert

That day, Jack and Daisy learned how to ride a camel. It was a bit like riding the waves in a tiny boat. You went up and down and up and down. But at least there was a saddle to hold on to, so Jack and Daisy got the hang of it very quickly.

Cousin Cedric was delighted.

The next day he tied two huge bunches of bananas on to his saddle.

"Essential provisions," he explained to Jack and Daisy as they climbed on to their camels. He grinned. "And bananas are my favourite!"

They set off across the desert. Soon there was nothing but sand and more sand.

Then something very odd happened.

Lightning flashed, thunder roared and suddenly torrents of rain poured out of a clear blue sky.

Within seconds Jack and Daisy and Cousin Cedric were soaked to the skin.

Within minutes their camels were stumbling up to their knees in puddles.

"What's happening?" shouted Jack and Daisy, wiping the rain from their eyes.

"Something very peculiar," replied Cousin Cedric in a strange voice. He held up the last banana. "Anyone hungry?"

"It's yours," said Jack and Daisy quickly. They never wanted to see a banana again.

As the sun went down, Jack and Daisy saw a magnificent stripy tent pitched beside an oasis. Glittering banners fluttered from its roof. Sweet-smelling smoke rose from its chimney.

"What's that?" yelled Jack over the pounding of the camel's hooves.

"That's where we're spending the night!" cried Cousin Cedric.

# 4. Delicious Crocodile Patties!

Cousin Cedric helped Jack and Daisy tie up their camels. Then they ducked under a flap and walked into the tent.

It was like walking into an Aladdin's cave!

Jack and Daisy had never seen

anything like it. Embroidered silk hangings and finely woven rugs covered the walls. Everything glowed in the light of brass lamps.

"Wow!" said Jack.

"Far out!" said Daisy.

"Shhh!" said Cousin Cedric.

A lady dressed in a flowing silver kaftan glided over the shining carpet. Ropes of yellow-and-red jewels glittered at her throat. She led Jack and Daisy into a small room and handed them each a pair of baggy pyjamas made out of gold cloth.

Daisy thought they were terrific.

Jack wasn't so sure.

When they had changed, the lady smiled the smallest of smiles.

"The feast is ready," she murmured. As she bowed, her necklaces made a soft tinkling sound.

A moment later, Jack and Daisy were sitting cross-legged at a long, low table.

"Whatever happens," whispered Cousin Cedric, "eat what's on your plate."

Jack and Daisy looked at the food. It was delicious. In fact, it was their favourite. Hamburgers, chips and marshmallows.

It was a bit strange to have marshmallows on the same plate, but Jack and Daisy were too hungry to care. Anyway, maybe that's what people did in Egypt.

When they had finished eating, an old man at the head of the table clapped his hands.

The lady in the silver kaftan appeared at his side and bowed low.

"Delicious crocodile patties," cried the old man.

"Loved the battered locusts," said someone else.

"Sheep's eyes were a triumph," added another.

Then they all smacked their lips loudly as if to say thank you.

Cousin Cedric looked sternly at Jack and Daisy. They did not have to be mind-readers to know what he was thinking.

And they had to admit everything had tasted better than school lunches.

For a moment, there was silence in the huge colourful tent.

Jack and Daisy grinned. Then they smacked their lips as well.

# 5. The Keeper of the Golden Key

It was as if a signal had been given. Suddenly Cousin Cedric jumped up from the table and stood in the middle of the room.

"Where are the Golden Bananas?" he cried.

"Um, no thanks," muttered Jack and Daisy, quickly.

But nobody seemed to notice.

The old man clapped his hands again and two bunches of tiny golden bananas were placed on the table.

Jack and Daisy were amazed. They looked as if they were made out of real gold.

"I am the Keeper of the Golden Bananas," announced the old man, solemnly. He stood up. "The Golden Bananas are the sacred offering to the Weather Monkey."

Jack and Daisy looked sideways at each other. What on earth was the old man talking about?

Then something even more extraordinary happened. Cousin Cedric stood up and bowed.

He held out a large golden key. "I am the Keeper of the Golden Key," he said. "The key to the Temple of the Weather Monkey."

Jack and Daisy couldn't believe their ears!

Their Cousin Cedric? Keeper of the Golden Key?

What on earth –?

"Arise, those wearing the Golden Pyjamas," cried the old man.

Nobody moved.

"Arise, those wearing the Golden Pyjamas," said the old man, again.

Jack and Daisy looked round the room. No one else was wearing golden pyjamas.

"Are you thinking what I'm thinking?" whispered Jack.

"Yup," replied Daisy.

So Jack and Daisy got up and stood beside Cousin Cedric in the middle of the room.

"Excellent!" cried the old man. "Now we have everybody we need."

He beamed and looked around him.

"As you know, the weather has been most peculiar recently," said the old man. A mutter of agreement went around the tent.

Cousin Cedric spoke. "This is because the Weather Monkey feels he is being ignored." He paused. "And when the Weather Monkey feels like that, he behaves extremely badly."

Cousin Cedric lifted the front flap of the tent.

Thick snow was falling outside.

A gasp of astonishment went through the room.

The old man bowed and looked serious. "It is written on the stones in the temple that two children must carry the Golden Bananas to the

Weather Monkey," he said. "It is further written that they must go with the Keeper of the Golden Key and they must keep this task *absolutely* secret."

The old man paused and looked Jack and Daisy in the eye. "Got it?" he said.

"Got it," replied Jack and Daisy.

"Excellent," cried the old man. He laid a bony hand on Cousin Cedric's shoulder. "There's no time to lose."

Cousin Cedric bowed. Then he lifted the bunches of tiny gold bananas and carefully put them in a leather pouch at his waist.

"We leave at dawn," said Cousin Cedric in a low voice.

# 6. This Is No Ordinary Monkey

It was a long and difficult journey. One minute the camels had to be fitted with snow shoes because the drifts were so deep. The next they had to wear water wings because the puddles had turned into lakes.

At last Jack and Daisy and Cousin Cedric arrived at what seemed like the end of the world. Empty land stretched away to meet the edge of the sky.

Except for one extraordinary thing.

Standing in the middle of nowhere, as if it had been dropped by a spaceship, was a huge yellow building made of stone.

It was the Temple of the Weather Monkey.

Jack and Daisy and Cousin Cedric climbed down from their camels and stretched their legs.

In the middle of the temple was a carved wooden door. Beside the door was an enormous egg timer.

"What's that for?" asked Jack, pointing to the egg timer.

"After I put the Golden Key in the door, we must turn the timer upside down before we go in," replied Cousin Cedric.

He looked worried as he fitted the great key in the lock.

"We have three minutes to go inside the temple, take the Golden Bananas to the Weather Monkey, and get out again."

"Why three minutes?" asked Jack.

Cedric smiled. "Because the Weather Monkey gets bored very

easily. He believes that anything that takes longer than three minutes is a waste of time."

"But what if it *does* take longer than three minutes?" asked Daisy, looking worried.

"Then the door will shut and we'll be locked inside," explained Cousin Cedric. He fixed Jack and Daisy with serious eyes. "And remember, no matter what you see or what you hear you mustn't laugh or you will be sucked back through the temple door and become slaves of the Weather Monkey, for ever."

"What's so funny about taking bananas to a monkey?" asked Daisy.

"These are no ordinary bananas," said Cousin Cedric. "And this is no ordinary monkey."

As he spoke he lifted the two tiny bunches of golden bananas from his pouch and handed one each to Jack and Daisy.

"Now listen carefully," said Cousin Cedric. "The altar to the Weather Monkey is in the middle of the temple. As soon as you see it place the bananas on top of it and *run*!"

Jack and Daisy took the bananas in both hands. Even though they were tiny they were quite heavy.

Suddenly the sky turned dark purple and a flash of lightning struck the egg timer.

It turned upside down and the first grains of sand slid through the middle.

"Oh no!" cried Cousin Cedric. "We're running out of time already!"

# 7. Burp! Grunt! Splat!

Cousin Cedric turned the key and yanked open the wooden door.

"Follow me!" he cried. Then he grabbed a flaming torch from the wall and ran down a long corridor.

Jack and Daisy raced after him as fast as they could.

There were paintings of monkeys, everywhere. And very silly paintings they were too.

There were monkeys dressed in fancy clothes. There were monkeys riding motorbikes. There were even monkeys water-skiing.

Jack and Daisy looked down at their feet and kept on going.

Suddenly the temple was full of voices making rude noises and telling terrible jokes.

*May I hold your hand?*

*No thanks, it isn't heavy.*

BURP!

*What did the Martian say to the petrol pump?*

*Take your finger out of your ear when I talk to you.*

GRUNT!

*What do you call a judge with no fingers?*

*Justice Thumbs.*

SPLAT!

*What do you give a sick pig?*

*Oinkment.*

YECH!

*What's the fastest thing on a washing line?*

*Hondapants.*

AARGH!

*What's the fastest thing in a river?*

*A motor-pike.*

PHUT!

It was almost impossible not to laugh.

# 8. Disaster Strikes!

Jack and Daisy stumbled down the corridor clutching their golden bananas. Their shoulders were shaking and they were pulling the most awful faces to stop themselves laughing.

At last they came to an

enormous room. A gigantic golden monkey stared down at them.

His eyes were crossed.

His tongue was sticking out.

His fingers were poked up his nose.

He was dancing from foot to foot with his toes turned in.

He looked *really* silly.

Cousin Cedric pointed frantically at his watch and then to the altar.

With a huge effort not to burst out laughing, Jack and Daisy lifted up the bananas and placed them on top.

Then they turned and ran after Cousin Cedric, still keeping their eyes firmly on their feet.

At the far end of the corridor,

the square of daylight was getting smaller.

The massive stone door was beginning to close!

Suddenly disaster struck!

Daisy looked up and saw a piece of paper pinned to the back of Cousin Cedric's long, flowing robe.

Scrawled across it were the words, I SMELL.

Daisy was almost out of the temple when she burst out laughing!

At that moment Daisy felt her pyjamas catch in the door. And sure enough she was being sucked back into the temple!

"Cousin Cedric!" yelled Jack. "Cousin Cedric!"

Quick as a flash, Cedric whipped out the curved sword he wore at his waist. He slashed through the baggy cloth of Daisy's golden pyjamas.

BANG! The huge stone door slammed shut. And half of Daisy's pyjamas were stuck inside for ever.

"That was a close shave!" cried Cousin Cedric. And they all started to laugh until tears poured down their cheeks.

# 9. A Thousand Thanks!

When Jack and Daisy stopped laughing and looked around them, they couldn't believe their eyes.

The snow had melted.

The sand was warm and dry.

A hot sun was shining out of a clear, blue sky.

The weather was normal again.

"A thousand thanks!" cried Cousin Cedric. As he spoke he climbed on to his camel and gathered up the reins of the other two. "I couldn't have done without you."

And before Jack and Daisy could even say goodbye, he thundered away across the desert.

"Jack and Daisy Primly-Proper?" said a voice. A limousine purred to a halt from behind the temple. A man with a friendly smile put his head out of the window. He had a thick black beard and a monkey sat on his shoulders.

"Amed!" cried Jack and Daisy.

Amed jumped out and opened the door of the limousine.

Jack and Daisy slid on to the vast back seat. Inside it was cool and there was a table of cold fizzy drinks and all kinds of crisps and chocolates.

"Compliments of your Cousin Cedric," laughed Amed. "He wishes you a safe journey home."

*

Mrs Primly-Proper was having a wonderful day. Mr Primly-Proper had strung up dozens of extra clothes lines all over the garden.

And every single one of them flapped with sheets and napkins and skirts.

Now that the sun was out again, Mrs Primly-Proper had washed

everything in the house at least twice.

Indeed, Mr Primly-Proper had only just managed to talk her out of dragging the three-piece suite into the garden and hosing it down with soapy water.

"Daisy!" cried Mrs Primly-Proper in dismay as she bent over the last basket of wet washing. "What on earth happened to those lovely gold pyjamas you brought back from Egypt?"

"They got caught in the door of the Great Temple," said Daisy with a grin.

"When we took the Golden Bananas to the Weather Monkey with Cousin Cedric," explained Jack.

"Don't talk nonsense, darlings," said Mrs Primly-Proper, primly.

"Supper's ready!" cried Mr Primly-Proper. "Hamburgers and chips. Marshmallows later."

"Crocodile patties and battered locusts," shouted Jack.

"Yum! Yum!" cried Daisy. "Sheep's eyes, my *favourite*!"

Mr Primly-Proper looked puzzled.

Mrs Primly-Proper looked peeved.

Jack and Daisy fell about laughing.